# The Magical Adventure of Little Alf

## The Enchanted Forest

Book

# By Hannah Louise Russell

# The Magical Adventure of Little Alf

## Book 2

Believe in magic and you will find

it...

# The Enchanted Forest

## Book 2

Follow Little Alf on his online blog! He has his own blog and Facebook page!

This way you can see all the exciting and cheeky things he gets up to at home! This also means you can watch out for where he is travelling to next!

If Little Alf is visiting a show near you then why not come and meet Little Alf and Hannah and get your book signed!


www.littlealf.com


Helping support the Riding for the Disabled Association.

\*\*\*

It had been nearly two whole months since Hannah had found Little Alf in the forest. Nobody knew where he had come from, but word soon spread that this tiny ball of fuzz had been found. People talked of the old stories and legends which were known in the forest many years ago.

Local newspapers and magazines had flocked to visit Little Alf. Nobody could understand how he had managed to survive the harshness of the previous winters in the damp forest; but he had, and it was a miracle.

Little Alf was soon to be known as the magic pony...

# Chapter One

It was a crisp winter's morning and the leaves crackled underneath Hannah's yellow wellies as she walked down the lane toward Meadowlea Stables. The trees were starting to look bare as the cold stripped away their leaves. The grass paddocks had a glimmer of crystal blue from the previous evening.

Crunch! Crackle!

Hannah turned and looked at Little Alf.

'Are you eating leaves again?' Hannah giggled as she looked into Little Alf's soft brown eyes. He snorted and shook his head as he grabbed another rusted leaf which had fallen from the solid tree through the autumn season.

'Oh! There you are Hannah, where have you been? We're going to be late!" said Hannah's Mum.

'I've been on a walk with Alf' said Hannah, as she tickled Alfie's ears.

'Well hurry up and put him in his paddock. I knew it was a bad idea letting you come up here before the fair' sighed Hannah's Mum.

'What fair..?' asked Hannah.

'Hannah! Leyburn Christmas Fair! I've been telling you about it all week! Now hurry up, and remember to wash your hands in the tack room. I hope you brought another pair of shoes. You can't go in your yellow wellies!'

Hannah blushed. 'I may have left them in the kitchen' she replied quietly.

'Well we've got no time to change now, we can't miss your Grandad's singing' said Mum.

Hannah giggled as she wandered back to Alfie's paddock.

She patted Alfie and gave him one last carrot before she turned and ran back to the car where her Mum was waiting with Sasha, their big golden and black German Shepherd. Hannah could faintly hear the low whinnying of Alfie as she closed the car door and wished she could be with him all the time. She always had a pang of guilt when she left him...

The market town of Leyburn was lined with people wrapped up in woolly hats and scarves, the car park overflowing with people resorting to parking in the Auction Mart. The

Christmas Fair was an amazing occasion, bringing people from all over the Dales into one place at the same time. There were craft stands, florists, bakery products and even a huge glittering silver ice rink set across the market place, where children, adults and teenagers were laughing as they slipped and glided over the frozen ice.

'There you are, Hannah! Where have you both been? You're going to miss your Grandad singing. Dad and John are already inside. Come on! We'd best hurry if we want to get a good seat' said Hannah's Nanna.

'I've been to see Little Alf' said Hannah, giggling.

'I know you have, you still have your wellies on!' said Nanna.

Leyburn Village Hall was full with people of all ages, and the sweet smell of freshly baked mince pies floated through the room. The hall was decorated with a huge Christmas tree, there were colourful green and red baubles covering the tree from top to bottom and a huge glittering silver star perched on top, while the silver flash of tinsel glittered brightly as the lights shone down and the candles glowed. Everybody settled in their seats. The lights were turned off and they were ready to listen to the Leyburn Choir.

\*\*\*

There was a huge roar of approval as the Choir took centre stage for one last song.

'Thank you to everyone who has attended Leyburn's Christmas Fair! I hope you all enjoy your day looking around the market place, and are ready for the special guest to appear and turn on the lights tonight!' said the organiser.

Everybody stood up in their seats and began to applaud as the curtains closed, the lights switched on, and people began to talk among themselves as ladies brought out steaming mince pies, mulled wine and hot chocolate.

'How's that young pony of yours doing then, Hannah?' said the man, as he stared down at her, sipping his mulled wine.

'Oh he's wonderful! I've just got him used to his head collar and being handled' replied Hannah, happily.

'Well, that's great; I bet it took a lot of time if he's never been handled before. I have Shetlands myself, and they can be a real handful! I've been reading all your progress in the local papers and magazines!' said the man.

'Little Alf seemed to like Hannah since day one, and hasn't left her side since!' said Hannah's mum. Hannah giggled shyly.

'Well that is a nice story! I work for a newspaper myself. I was wondering - since he's all everybody talks about - whether we could do an article on you and Little Alf!' asked the man.

'Wow, really! Of course you can!' Hannah beamed.

'I'll look forward to working with you then' the man said, as he passed Hannah one of his business cards.

Hannah smiled happily. 'It really is beginning to feel like Christmas' Hannah thought to herself, as she wandered into the town to find Tilly.

Tilly had been Hannah's friend since she moved to the Yorkshire Dales, and had helped Hannah find Little Alf when nobody else believed her; if it wasn't for Tilly she might never have been able to catch him. It was Tilly's idea to leave a trail of carrots to Meadowlea Stables, and luckily Little Alf followed through the night and had arrived at the stables the next morning.

'There you are Tilly! I've been looking for you everywhere' said Hannah.

'Well you didn't look very hard did you! I've been here all along!' giggled Tilly.

'Well I can't have then!' said Hannah, laughing.

'Have you tried out the ice skating rink yet?' asked Tilly.

'No, I was never very good at it before, I always fall over' replied Hannah.

'That's part of the fun! Come on, we have to try it! It won't be here until next year' replied Tilly excitedly.

'Okay then' Hannah sighed.

The sun shined down and the ice rink glittered as Hannah and Tilly gingerly stepped on the ice.

# Chapter Two

Hannah moaned as she reached to turn her alarm clock off. 'Why did I agree to ice skate yesterday?' she thought to herself as she looked at the huge black and purple bruise which had formed in the middle of her forehead overnight.

Hannah pulled on her crinkled brown jodhpurs and mud stained blue sweatshirt, she was ready to spend her whole day at Meadowlea Stables; she couldn't wait to see Alfie again. The light shone through her curtains as she pulled them back and was surprised to see there was a crisp thin layer of snow. She trudged downstairs, yawning, and was welcomed by Maggie the golden Cocker spaniel.

'HAHAHAHA, what happened to your head!' laughed Hannah's older brother, John. Hannah frowned and rubbed her forehead.

'That *is* a nasty bruise' said Hannah's Dad, as he lowered his newspaper. Hannah pulled down her grey woolly hat.

'There. Nobody will be able to see my bruise now' Hannah thought to herself. Meadowlea Stables always looked glorious in the morning, and Hannah still got butterflies in her tummy the moment she arrived. The horses were rugged up and happily munching their hay. Hannah jumped out of the car and slipped on the ice.

'Be careful Hannah, there's black ice everywhere. It was very cold last night' Ruth, the owner of the stables, called. Hannah smiled as she clutched the door handle of the car before gingerly stepping over to the frosted grass.

'Have a good day Hannah. I'll see you tonight' said her Mum, waving through the car window.

'Thank you Mum, see you later!' Hannah called.

***

'Alfie! Alfie!'

'Alfie, where are you!' shouted Hannah, worriedly.

'He might be small, but he's not that small' Hannah thought to herself. She scrambled over the frozen mud, and climbed onto the large tree trunk which had fallen down months ago. She stood up on her tiptoes and called for Alfie but there was no movement... no sound... just silence.

Hannah began to panic as Alfie was nowhere to be seen...

# Chapter Three

Hannah quickly ran towards the gate, fearing she may never see Alfie again, and bolted up towards the stables where she had seen Ruth go earlier. She quickly barged past through the door, breathless.

'He's gone!' Hannah sobbed.

'He's not there' she said, before tears began to run down her rosy cheeks.

'What's happened, Hannah? Come on, you look shaken up' said Ruth.

'What's the matter, Hannah?' Tilly asked.

'Alfie isn't in his paddock. He's gone! I may never see him again' Hannah cried.

'Oh, this is my fault' said Ruth. Hannah looked at Ruth worriedly.

'I put him in a stable last night. I knew it was going to be frosty, so I didn't want him catching a cold. Sorry, I completely forgot to tell you earlier when I saw you' sighed Ruth.

'You mean he's in here, he's okay?' smiled Hannah.

'Of course he's okay Hannah, although he's been screaming the place down all morning waiting for you' replied Tilly. There was suddenly a huge high-pitched whinny.

'There we go! You'd best go see him' Ruth said.

Hannah giggled as she ran down the barn towards his stable.

***

'Alfie! You're here! ' Hannah shouted in joy, as she crouched down to give Alfie a kiss on his nose. Alfie shook his head and snorted, as Hannah produced a carrot from her pocket.

'Do you want to go play in the ménage today Alf? I've even brought my camera. I thought I could take some photos and show my cousin Maria this weekend, she's coming to stay for a few days! What do you think?' Hannah giggled as she stroked Alfie.

'If you're going to the ménage Hannah, just be very careful. It's still very icy outside and I don't want either of you getting injured just before Christmas' said Ruth, as she passed Alfie's stable.

'We'll be super careful, won't we, Alf!' Hannah said, as Alfie snorted and nudged her pocket for one more carrot. She opened the stable door and headed to the tack room to get Alfie's head collar. The old tack room was one of Hannah's favourite places to be. It wasn't like any normal tack room, it had posters lining the wooden walls and old horse books on a book shelf made out of silver horse shoes. Hannah also loved the strong smell of leather as soon as she entered, and her most favourite thing of all was the quote on the back of the wooden door, in very faint black letters which said...

'Believe in magic, and you will find it...'

Underneath was a drawing of a huge oak tree.

*Believe in magic and you will find it...*

Hannah hadn't noticed the quote when she had first visited the stables at Meadowlea but once she had started to use the tack room more after finding Alfie, every time she stepped into the old wooden room, Hannah got a very twinkly feeling in her belly, and she almost wanted to believe it *was* magic. She was just about to step outside when she glanced at the quote one last time. She could have sworn it glowed... She was soon met by the frosty cool air as she closed the tack room door and gingerly headed back towards the stables.

***

Alfie rolled, bucked and screamed as he ran around the ménage. Hannah giggled. He was just so excited to be out in the sand, and she took photo after photo while Alfie jumped off from all four feet and sprinted from one side of the ménage to the other.

Alfie squealed and bucked, before stopping and watching something through the dark wooden bars of the fencing. Hannah slowly got up from her crouched position and wandered over next to Alfie.

'What can you see, boy?' Hannah said, as she patted Alfie's neck. She scanned the area but all she could see was miles of frosted silver fields and the mysterious forest where she had first found Little Alf. Alfie let out a high-pitched whinny and began pacing the fence, creating a path in the sandy floor.

'Is Alfie okay, Hannah? We could hear him from the yard' shouted Lucy, one of the stable girls, who was now standing by the ménage fence.

'He *was* okay. He just seems to be a bit unsettled now' replied Hannah, as she glanced at Alfie.

'Maybe he's seen another horse or something in the distance!' shouted Lucy.

'I can't see anything' replied Hannah, confused. Alfie then stopped whining and ran over to her and nudged her pockets. Hannah giggled.

'You certainly know where your carrots are kept don't you!' Hannah laughed, giving him a carrot. As she gently put Alfie's head collar over his nose and buckled his strap ready to go back to his outside paddock for the day, she still wondered what had unsettled him earlier. Was he trying to tell her something...? She sometimes found Alfie in his field staring towards the mysterious forest and often wondered if Alfie wished he was still there. She knew their bond was extremely strong, so why would Alfie want to go back?

***

Once Hannah had put Alfie back in his stable she headed into the kitchen. As soon as she opened the door she was hit with the strong smell of coffee; the kitchen was always a great place to be at lunch time, with everyone sitting round the large handmade wooden bench which could seat over twenty people, while the fire roared behind them. Terry,

the Jack Russell puppy, bounded up onto Hannah's legs as she sat down next to Tilly.

'Hot chocolate, cream and marshmallows, Hannah?' asked Ruth.

'Oh course, my favourite!' replied Hannah, laughing.

'We know!' said everyone around the table.

Hannah laughed as she began to tuck into her homemade sandwiches.

'Where are we going riding this afternoon then, Ruth?' asked Grace, one of the girls who rode at Meadowlea Stables.

'I think we're going to go into the mysterious forest, but as always we'll have to see what mood the horses are in. The wooden bridge may be very icy today so we might go down the usual bridleway' replied Ruth, as she applied the marshmallows to Hannah's hot chocolate. The group groaned. Ruth laughed.

'Well we will try going into the mysterious forest but health and safety come first, remember'. The group cheered.

'I love the forest in winter, the way the birds sing and the holly and berries glisten on the leaves' said Tilly, excitedly.

'I love the way the sun beams through the trees best. It makes it so enchanted and magical' said Hannah.

'I'll always remember the herd of wild deer we once saw, now that *was* magical' said Lucy.

'Well my Dad said only this morning that the forest might not be there for much longer' said Toby, the sandy-haired boy who kept his horse at Meadowlea.

'What do you mean?' asked Hannah, confused.

'They say the forest doesn't get used anymore so they're going to use it for bigger things such as building and modern resources. They're going to use the wood for furniture and paper, that's what my Dad says' said Toby.

'They can't do that! We use it for riding, it's a bridleway' said Hannah, shocked at this news.

'I'm afraid they can Hannah. They filed a registration form of submission against it, there isn't much we can do. There's nothing to stop them' sighed Ruth.

'But what about our cross country course and bridleway?' said Tilly, alarmed.

'I'm not too sure, but we still have the other bridleways' answered Ruth.

Hannah sighed, she loved the mysterious forest and the enchanted stream, the way it changed colour in the seasons, and most of all it was where she had the memories of finding Alfie. It would look bare without the forest, but what could she do...?

# Chapter Four

'Paddy, stop nudging me, I can't do your girth' Hannah sighed, as she struggled to pull it up to the saddle. Paddy shook his head excitedly before letting out a huge whinny.

'Is everyone tacked up and ready?' Ruth shouted.

'Yes' the group chorused.

'No. I'm not. Paddy's girth won't meet his saddle' Hannah cried down the yard. Ruth walked down the yard to meet Hannah at her stable door.

'Oh no, it looks to me that Paddy's been eating a lot recently, looks like we'll have to cut down his feed!' Ruth said. Hannah giggled while Ruth fastened the girth.

'Right. Now Paddy's sorted, we'll all mount our horses and ponies and set off up the bridleway towards the mysterious forest' Ruth shouted.

There was a loud cheer as the group headed towards the mounting block. Hannah gathered her reins and Paddy lifted his head, snorted and began to prance on the spot. Hannah always loved going to the mysterious forest. It was as if all the horses knew too, because they would always begin to prance and swish their tails in excitement.

As they rode down the yard the horses left in the paddocks would canter and scream, while the cows came to greet them by the fence. Alfie neighed as Hannah passed his paddock.

'See you soon Alfie!' she shouted. She never liked leaving him. Alfie would neigh for ages after Hannah left, especially when she was going in the direction of the forest... Alfie took off, galloping round his field kicking and frantically swishing his head and jumping off from all four feet. Hannah giggled; she loved to watch him play in his field. They had tried to put Paddy, Badger and Pepper, three gelding from the stables into the paddock with Alfie to keep him company, but Alfie had tried to escape in panic so they made the decision to keep them separate to avoid injury. Hannah would hate Alfie to get injured for no reason.

The group trotted up the dusty path, the horses' hooves elegantly gliding through the fallen rustic leaves, the leather on the saddles squeaking as the riders settled in to their horse's bouncy rhythms.

'Steady, boy' Hannah said, as she patted Paddy's neck. Paddy always wanted to go faster, swishing his head and snorting loudly, but he soon began to settle into a comfortable rhythm. Hannah often admired Paddy's grace; he was one of the most magnificent horses she had ever seen, and she often watched him in his paddock at Meadowlea. He would show his pride by prancing with his ears straight forward, nostrils flaring, tail up and head pointing downwards on his arched neck.

He would always show his eagerness at new objects by stamping his front foot followed by his hind, shaking his head and almost dancing sideways. Hannah had learnt through watching Paddy that he would often shake his head more often than any other horse she had ever known, and when she studied the horse books she got from the library, she narrowed it down to Paddy being excited. Although every horse was different, Hannah knew when she read it that it was right. He was always the first lined up in his paddock ready and waiting to go out on a ride, and would often neigh when someone approached him.

***

All the horses began to swish their tails and surge forward toward the twinkling trees. Ruth approached the forest on her large dark bay Friesian, nudging her horse on to the narrow wooden bridge, which was now covered in a slimy camouflage green moss. The bridge sparkled in the sun where the ice was still shimmering from the early morning frost.

'Can everyone gather round, please!' Ruth shouted towards the riders. The group nudged their horses on, creating a circle around where Ruth was sitting on her Friesian.

'The bridge hasn't defrosted like I'd hoped for so we'll be taking another path...' Ruth explained. The group groaned; the forest was the most enchanting and exhilarating place to be at Meadowlea Stables and there were jumps set up among the forest trees where the riders would take it in turn to fly over one by one.

'Wait a minute before you all start groaning! I was going to suggest we jump the stream carefully, you've all been jumping now for at least a year so if you ever came to a situation such as a fallen tree you would have to jump the tree if there was no way home, so we're going to safely and carefully jump the stream. I'll go first, followed by Jack and Tilly. We all know Jack loves to jump, so he can lead the rest of you through', Ruth shouted as she watched the grins spread across the children's faces. Hannah suddenly felt a pang of nerves, and glanced at the stream worriedly. It wasn't wide but it was deep, and one wrong move could land her in a pit of slime and mud.

Paddy began to jig-jog on the spot, eager to follow the other horses to the other side... It was a tense moment as Tilly made the first jump over, Hannah held her breath as Tilly landed gracefully on the other side. It was now time for Hannah to jump. She turned Paddy in a short circle and nudged him on towards the edge, gathering up her reins and leaning forward ready to jump...

Hannah could feel Paddy's body tense as they transitioned into a canter, then he snorted and stopped dead just before the steep edge, sending Hannah forward, clutching her arms around Paddy's neck.

'Are you okay, Hannah?' shouted Ruth.

'Yeah, I'm fine. He just got a bit tense as we went into canter' Hannah said, as she sat up in her saddle and gathered up the reins again. She took a deep breath as she spun Paddy around and nudged him back to canter in a large circle before heading back towards the edge of the stream. This time, as they got nearer to the stream, she clutched onto Paddy's mane, more determined than ever to make it to the other side; she did not want to miss going into the forest today. Paddy raised his two front feet off the ground,Hannah threw herself into a forward jump position, holding her breath. She knew it was going to be tight. Paddy had jumped too early...

His two hooves landed on the edge of the other side of the bank. Hannah thought she was safe and let out a huge sigh of relief, but then Paddy began to scramble. His hind feet where hanging off the edge, threatening to fall backwards at any moment. Hannah gritted her teeth. She was not going to let either of them get injured. She kicked him on, encouraging him to fight to get up the bank. Paddy scrambled, sending rocks into the deep stream below.

'Come on, Paddy!' Hannah cried, as she tightened her grip around his mane. She thought he had given up. His body sank tired, he began to slide backwards, but just when she thought Paddy had given up, he bolted forward, sending the bank into an avalanche of grass, mud and dirt. Hannah let out a huge sigh of relief as they made it to the other side, patting Paddy and wrapping her arms around his neck in a tight hug.

'Well done Paddy!, Good boy!' Hannah whispered in a soothing voice. Paddy was breathing heavily, tired from the effort of getting up the bank.

'That was amazing!' shouted Toby, sitting onTeddy, the black Shetland.

'That was scary!' shouted Tilly.

'Well done, Hannah,that was very well sat! Most people would have fallen on his first refusal' said Ruth.

'He did very well; it was my mistake I pushed him to jump too early' said Hannah, frustrated that she could have injured her horse.

'Well, we all make mistakes, but you didn't do anything much wrong. Paddy just lost his footing near the end of the jump, otherwise he jumped very gracefully' replied Ruth.

'Well at least they're both okay! Can we get going now? Jack's getting restless' Tilly said, excited to be going into the forest.

'Come on then, everyone follow Jack down the path. Sure you're okay, Hannah?' Ruth asked,concerned Hannah may be shocked from the event.

'Of course I am. It was pretty thrilling! I was just worried about Paddy' Hannah giggled.

The group headed down the dirty path which was now covered in a thin layer of green glistering moss. The trees swayed as a light gust of wind blew through the crooked branches, the forest was full of colours, there were orange and red leaves which had fallen off the trees, leaving the branches looking bare and wilted. There was a strong smell of wild winter flowers and the rotting wood from the damp broken twigs lying in the undergrowth among the humming insects and the rustle of the animals below. The horse's feet crunched through the leaves as they headed deeper into the forest.

Hannah had a sudden twinkling feeling in her belly just like before, reading the quote from the wooden tack room door. As she rode into the forest she remembered when she had first heard Alfie and had been more determined than ever to prove he was real. She smiled at the thought of finding him, remembering the first time she saw him, his hair all matted, and his feet overgrown, but their bond had almost been instant. The moment she had looked into his large soft brown eyes she had known Alfie was meant for her, and in the past few months of spending time with Alfie the bond was stronger than ever...

'Right, team. I think we'll have a rest and something to eat, all the horses have worked hard today; battling through the mud is tiring work, so if you would all like to dismount and let your horses munch the grass for a while, we'll have a little snack! I've brought hot chocolate, biscuits, and apples for the horses! Then we'll mount up and head home to Meadowlea' Ruth said, as she began to hand the children their snacks. Hannah and Tilly dismounted their horses and carefully sipped the steaming hot chocolate. There was still a light glistening frost on the ground as the horses searched for fresh grass.

\*\*\*

Hannah was watching Paddy as he snatched at the fresh grass he had found underneath a large solid oak tree which still held its green leaves.

'How strange' she muttered to herself. All the trees in the forest had lost their leaves but this one's still shone brightly as the sun bounced off them. As she got near to the tree, she suddenly felt dizzy and her tummy began with the twinkly feeling she had felt earlier that day. She reached out and touched the rough tree bark.

Hannah gasped and jumped back as a sudden shock travelled down her finger. Golden dust flashed around her hand, leaving her wondering what had just happened. She looked back towards Paddy and he was still happily eating his grass. Had that just been a dream...?

Hannah reached out and touched the tree again; it almost beckoned her to touch it, she couldn't resist. She leaned forward and reached out, placing her palm on the tree. This time Hannah felt a twinkling feeling, like magic swirling around her body; the golden dust started to form around her, creating swirls of gold and silver; then she was suddenly thrown to the right by a strange force, landing on the tree's twisted roots.

However, she was not hurt at all, and felt as if light was travelling through her body. Happiness spread over her as she watched the golden dust magically dance around the bottom of the old tree trunk. Then she saw something glowing, crawling over to the bottom of the tree and clawing the dead leaves out of the way, she saw, in tiny letters formed out of the wooden bark...

'Believe in magic and you will find it...'

Hannah gasped. 'What could that mean?' she thought to herself. She looked over to Ruth and the rest of the riders, who had now begun to mount their horses. Had anyone else seen? She glanced down to read the bark one last time, but this time there was nothing there...

 # Chapter Five

 Hannah stumbled towards Paddy, unsure of what had just happened, and whether it was all just a dream. She carefully gathered up Paddy's reins and mounted into the saddle. Paddy snorted and shook his head, before prancing over to the rest of the group ready to head back to the stables. As Hannah rejoined the rest of the group they were all laughing and talking together.

'They must not have seen anything', Hannah thought, wondering what she *had* just seen, 'Could it be real? Is it possible?' she muttered to herself.

'Sorry Hannah. Were you asking me something? I didn't hear you' Tilly smiled at Hannah.

'Oh no, sorry. I was just thinking out loud' Hannah said, suddenly brought back to reality as a light breeze pricked her skin, sending a shiver across her body, giving her goose bumps.

'Right, team. I can see the warmth of the hot chocolate is starting to wear off so we'd best head back now. We'll take the shortcut across the fields, trot across the first one and a steady canter across the second. Ready? Let's go!' Ruth signalled her horse to go into a forward trot.

Hannah looked back towards the large oak tree one last time; the green leaves shone and glistened in the sun, and Hannah could have sworn she saw a golden ball of dust dancing around the tree...

***

After Hannah had returned Paddy to his stable and fed him for the night, she wandered out to collect Alfie from his field. He was waiting patiently by his gate. The orange sun was beginning to set as Hannah led Alfie into his warm stable for the night. She sighed as she patted him.

'Alfie, you will not believe what happened today. I was in the enchanted forest and there was a huge oak tree, still covered in fresh green leaves, and there was a surge of golden pixie dust. It was beautiful and enchanting and I got a sudden twinkly feeling pass over me. I think it was magic'

Alfie pricked his ears listening to Hannah.

'But it must have been a dream, it must, it's like something out of a fairy tale, it can't be real, can it?' Hannah said, frustrated as she wanted to believe she had seen the words carved in the bottom of the tree, but if it *was* real then nothing made sense. Why would the same words on the tack room door be carved into an old oak tree? The only thing that Hannah knew was every time she read the words out loud she got a very strong magical feeling...

Alfie rested his head on Hannah's lap as she sat against his stable door. She stroked his soft brown face as he nuzzled his head against her and his soft brown eyes looked into hers.

'What do you think, Alf? *Was* it all a dream?' Hannah wondered out loud.

Alfie squealed and shook his head as he excitedly leapt off from all four feet. 'Is that a no, then?' Hannah giggled. Alfie snorted and nudged her pocket, waiting for his carrot. She heard her mum talking to Ruth outside and knew it was time to go home. She kissed Alfie on the nose and ruffled his mane.

'Night, Alf' Hannah whispered as she glanced at the little ball of fluff before heading out the stable door. As she left she saw something glittering out of the corner of her eye, just like she had seen in the forest. She hesitated and wandered back to Alfie's stable, but when she got there he was sleeping peacefully. Hannah shook her head,

'I must be tired' she muttered as she walked outside to meet her Mum.

'Bye, Ruth. Thank you for today' Hannah said, as she jumped into the car. They drove out of the lane and down the steady track that lead up to Meadowlea Stables.

'Did you have a good day then, Hannah, you've been very quiet?' her Mum asked.

'Yes, it was really good. I groomed Alfie and took him for a walk. He screamed like mad when I went out riding with Paddy and left him' Hannah said, smiling.

'He must have wanted to join in!' said Mum.

'Either that or go to the forest...' Hannah said, wondering out loud.

'Now, why would he want to do that? Everyone can see how much he adores you; he wouldn't want to go back!' Her Mum was surprised that Hannah could think that Alfie wanted to go back to the forest when everyone knew how strong the bond between them was. Hannah was the only one who could catch Alfie for months.

'I don't know, I know we have a really strong bond and I love him so much but I always find him looking towards the forest' Hannah sighed. She couldn't stand the thought of losing Alfie.

'Well maybe he's just curious' said her Mum.

'Maybe' Hannah said, but something told her she was wrong.

They arrived back at their large country house, Hannah loved the new house. They had moved in almost seven months ago, but Hannah couldn't believe how fast this time had gone. She was greeted by Sasha and Maggie, the family dogs, and the high pitched squeak from Hannah's guinea pigs Candy and Floss welcomed them as they walked into the quaint wooden kitchen.

Just then, Hannah noticed, as she glanced into the mirror, that the large purple bruise which had been spread across her forehead had gone. She blinked and began to study her face. This morning when she had gone downstairs her brother John had teased her about the huge lump and purple bruise on her head from ice skating with Tilly the previous day, but the bruise was no longer there... Was it possible that the magic from the tree had healed her bruise?

Hannah soon realised how silly that would sound if she tried to explain to someone that the tree had healed her bruise. She decided that she had to go back to the exact spot the following weekend and find out for herself.

***

The school week went slowly and all Hannah could think about was the mysterious forest she loved so much. She thought it must all have been a dream, but something was tugging in the back of her mind telling her to go back once more.

'Are you going riding this weekend, Hannah?' asked Tilly, standing next to Hannah holding her guitar. Tilly had music practice twice a week, Hannah always admired the way Tilly was with music, and she was a great singer too.

'Not sure... I want to check something out with Alfie so I might just groom him and go on a long walk towards the forest or something' Hannah said, not sure how much to tell Tilly.

'I hope you're not thinking Alfie wants to go back to the forest again, he loves his stable! When I pass with Jack he's always waiting for you to come' replied Tilly, giggling.

Hannah laughed. 'I know, he never wants to go out in the morning either, I think he'd love to live in permanently'

'I think you're right' Tilly said, laughing.

'Where do you think we'll ride when the forest isn't there?' said Toby, who rode at Meadowlea and attended Thornberry Primary school with Tilly and Hannah.

'Oh, I don't know. I love the forest' Tilly said sighing.

'Me too!' huffed Toby.

Hannah's eyes widened, she had completely forgotten about the forest soon being chopped down, and suddenly felt a horrible feeling wash over her just like the magical feeling she got when talking about the forest, but this time it was bad. Hannah knew she had to find out what was in the forest and how she could help to stop it being chopped down.

'Are you okay, Hannah, you don't look very well?' said the Maths teacher, Mr Brown.

'Yes, I'm okay' Hannah said, although she didn't feel okay at all. She was feeling very sad about the forest going. It was where she had found Alfie and where all her memories were since moving. It was her most favourite thing about Meadowlea Stables and she couldn't stand the thought of not being able to ride through the bridlepaths or jump over the broken down trees, or even splash through the stream in the hot days of summer...

'Do you think there is any way we can stop them chopping the forest down? It would be a real shame, there's loads of wildlife in the forest, they'll be left with nowhere to live' Tilly said.

'I'm not sure really. My Dad said that the National Park ends just before the forest, so if you apply it can be built on, or used for modern resources. There used to be old documents and papers about the forest in the Town Hall Library, but they were caught in the fire last year and there are no other records, so it's up to whoever owns the land, I suppose' replied Toby.

'Looks like we'll just be going across the fields then' Tilly sighed. Hannah was sitting looking out of the huge bay window, planning her weekend's adventure with Alfie when she heard the old school bell ringing. The children jumped out of their seats and rushed towards the dinner hall. Thornberry Primary School was not a modern school at all. The windows leaked, the paint was chipped and they still had old fashioned desks, but all the children seemed to love it.

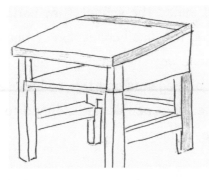

It was a very small school with only fifty students attending, but this never seemed to affect anyone and made it more of a community. Hannah had picked Thornberry School when she first arrived. Her parents had given her the choice of two, and Thornberry seemed more inviting and friendly to her than the others. Hannah had also met Tilly at Meadowlea Stables before she started school, and they had been best friends ever since.

'Ewww I hate mash, especially when it has huge lumps in' Tilly said, as she poked it with her fork. Hannah giggled.

'I think I'll stick with my packed lunch, my Mum makes the best sandwiches!' Hannah said as she took a huge bite.

'You're so lucky! My parents are usually working so it's easier for me to have school dinners' said golden-haired Lizzie.

'Do you want to go to the library after lunch and read some horse books?' Tilly asked excitedly.

'Of course' Hannah said, slightly surprised that Tilly needed to ask her. Since Hannah and Tilly had met at the stables and Hannah had joined the school, they had spent every lunchtime reading the small collection of horse books the library held. There was one particular book that Hannah loved; it was of old legends and tales of horses that had once lived, horses that people had claimed to be talented, intelligent and even magic...

# Chapter Six

Hannah jumped out of bed and changed quickly, jumping over the pile of dirty clothes in the hallway and running down the cluttered stairs without pausing, her bare feet drumming against the creaking floor. She burst into the kitchen, out of breath, startling her family who were all happily eating their breakfast, her Dad sitting reading the local paper, her Mum knitting a purple scarf and her brother with his head down and hands under the table, sneakily feeding Maggie, the Cocker spaniel.

'What's the matter, Hannah?' her Mum stood up, looking a little worried. Hannah gasped, holding up her finger, signalling her Mum to give her a minute to get her breath back.

'I'm late! It's already 9 o clock! I need to get to the stables' said Hannah, excitedly.

'Sorry Hannah, not today. I rang Ruth last night and she's going to check Alfie this morning and put him in his paddock because we have to get you some new shoes for school and your brother needs some new clothes, he's outgrown his others, and we're also going to call in at your Nanna's and pick up the mince pies she's made for us, and then tonight you can go see Alfie and put him to bed before it gets dark' said her Mum, as she picked up her knitting needles and set to work on the purple scarf.

'But Mum... I had plans, and Alfie won't want anyone else to put him outside today... 'Hannah said, sulking and thinking about the forest. She'd been looking forward to going to Meadowlea all week, planning the route she would take with Alfie and explaining it to him. He would be disappointed as well, Hannah thought to herself.

'Well you can spend the whole day there tomorrow' said Hannah's Dad, who had now put down the newspaper and was digging into his freshly made bacon sandwich.

'But I wanted to go today, Tilly won't be there tomorrow, please can I go... please...? 'Hannah begged.

'No. You're coming with us whether you like it or not, now hurry up and get your breakfast. We're going soon' said Hannah's mum, tidying the breakfast plates away. Hannah slowly munched her breakfast, thinking of Alfie waiting for her all day.

***

The day had gone slowly and Hannah was tired from walking round all the shops looking for new shoes, but they had finally settled on a pair of black boots for school, not something Hannah would usually wear, but she just wanted to get to the stables and see Alfie.

They finally headed up the steep path towards Meadowlea Stables, and Hannah got a tingly feeling in her stomach.

'Right Hannah we'll be back in an hour, have a good time!' her Dad shouted as he began to drive away down the dusty path.

## 'STOP! WAIT!'

Hannah heard someone shouting from the grass paddock. Her Dad stopped the car halfway up the path and began to turn around back towards the stables. She turned her head to see a large group of people running up the paddock towards her. She suddenly got a very uneasy feeling and began to search for Alfie in his paddock...

'He's not there, Hannah' Lucy, the stable girl said, as she reached Hannah.

'What do you mean he's not there, where is he?' Hannah began to panic.

'We're not sure, we've been looking for a few hours, we're just about to search the other fields now, he can't have gone too far, don't worry' Ruth said, holding a bag of carrots, but Hannah could tell Ruth was worried.

'What do you mean, how long has he been missing, where has he gone?' Hannah said, alarmed as she began to scan the area for Alfie.

'We're not sure, I put him in his paddock this morning, he seemed restless but I just presumed it was because you weren't here this morning, and when I went to check him this afternoon he was gone, but there was no trace of how he could have got out' said Ruth, concerned.

'Has he been stolen?' Hannah cried out, now in tears.

'We're really not sure, but he'll be around here somewhere' Ruth said. Hannah's Dad parked the car and her whole family came rushing over. Tears ran down Hannah's cheeks; she couldn't bear the thought of losing Alfie forever. Ruth quickly explained to her Mum, Dad and brother what had happened, and they quickly arranged a plan to search the local area, there was only an hour of light left as the sky had now changed to a hazy orange. If they were going to find Alfie today they had to hurry, as they were running out of light...

'Alfie! Alfie, where are you?' Hannah shouted as she trekked across the boggy field, the light was slowly beginning to fade. The whole group had split into two groups of four and all gone in different directions to search.

'I don't think he's this way' shouted Hannah's Dad through the wind.

'We'll just look a bit longer' Hannah cried. She had to find Alfie tonight, she had to. Her Dad's phone began to ring as she squinted her eyes towards the trees. Then she realised that, if Alfie had escaped, the only place he would go was the forest...

She suddenly began to sprint as fast as she could towards the forest; it was a race against light...

'Hannah, Hannah where you going?' her Dad shouted, struggling to keep up behind her. She ignored her Dad and carried on running, but the darkness was fast coming down in front of her as a deep mist began to cover the fields ahead. Hannah stopped, unsure of where she was, squinting against the darkness. A firm hand suddenly gripped her on the shoulder and she screamed in fright.

'Hannah, it's only me, we have to head back now or we'll get lost as well' said her Dad.

'But... what about Alfie?' Hannah replied as the tears fell once more.

'We will find him tomorrow, I'm sure' said her Dad as he wrapped her arms around Hannah.

'But what if I never see him again? I think he's in the forest, please Dad can I go look? You can go back and get a torch and meet me there. Please?' she said, pleading to him.

'Sorry Hannah, it's too dangerous. If you're sure he's in the forest we'll gather everyone tomorrow. He can't have gone that far' replied her Dad, soothingly. Hannah glanced at the forest through the darkness and reluctantly began to head back towards Meadowlea Stables.

As they got back, everyone was hugging Hannah and telling her how sorry they were, and they would find Alfie tomorrow for sure, but she couldn't help but think about Alfie out in the cold all night. Decembers in North Yorkshire were known to be very cold and in the past few weeks there had been snow and high winds. Hannah slowly slid into the car and headed home. She knew Alfie must be in the forest but she didn't know where. She clutched onto his head collar as they headed down the steep hill home...

# Chapter Seven

Hannah was ready the next morning to go in search of Little Alf. She hadn't slept at all the night before, and once they got home the rain had begun to lash down, first of all it had been a light pitter-patter against the windows, but it wasn't long until the rain turned to thunder and lightning, and very soon it was pelting down. Hannah couldn't eat that night, she was so worried about Alfie; but today she was ready to find him, and she was almost certain he was in the forest.

She was wrapped up with her yellow wellingtons on, waterproof trousers, rainproof coat, and a rucksack full of carrots and Alfie's head collar. She was ready to get Alfie and bring him back to Meadowlea. Every time she thought about the forest and Alfie she got the same tingly feeling she had felt previously... 'Could this be linked?' Hannah kept thinking to herself, but she had no time to waste. She had to find him today.

'Right come on then, we have a pony to find' said Hannah's Mum as the whole family got in the car and headed to Meadowlea stables. When they arrived there was the whole team waiting, Hannah's tears soon began to fall, all these people had come to find Alfie with her, and she couldn't believe it. There were the local owners from shops, farms and restaurants, the local newspaper team and the whole yard from Meadowlea Stables. As they pulled into the yard Hannah jumped out of the car and ran over to where Tilly was standing next to Ruth.

'Any news?' Hannah said, hoping.

'No, sorry Hannah, but we will find him, look at all the people who've come to help. The shops have all closed today, once they heard Alfie had gone missing, and the local paper, they thought they could do a missing article for him. We will find him, don't worry' replied Ruth.

Hannah smiled weakly at all the people who had come to search for him. Everyone parted into their teams, exchanging numbers and agreeing to meet around 2pm if nobody had any news. Ruth and a group of riders decided to take the horses and ride across the fields to cover more ground, while Hannah, her parents and her brother John decided to set towards the enchanted forest.

As they got nearer towards the forest, Hannah got the magical feeling in her body; she knew Alfie was in the forest and she knew where to find him. Once they had reached the forest, all four of Hannah's family members decided to split up to cover the area in enough time.

As soon as Hannah was out of sight of her parents, she began to sprint in the direction of the oak tree, the same oak tree where she thought she saw the words...

  'Believe in magic and you will find it'

and the same oak tree where she was almost certain she saw the golden magic dust...

 Hannah slipped on the muddy ground and landed face down on the woodland floor. She groaned as she slowly got up. Her ankle was sore and her wrist was already beginning to bruise, she looked down at her grazed knee and ripped trousers. Her yellow wellingtons were now a muddy brown colour and blended with the broken twigs of the trees and the dying leaves. She slowly began to walk, less swiftly this time, taking more care, she knew the old oak tree was just around the corner. Her ankle was now beginning to feel tight and swollen as she walked through the forest, but she didn't care. Her main focus was to find Alfie.

\*\*\*

Hannah slipped through the branches of the forest trees and into the open, and there it was - the large oak tree.

She hadn't noticed before but it towered above the rest of the trees, and it was wider than any tree she had ever seen

before, the leaves still a lush green with birds nestling happily among the branches... 'This must be a dream' she thought to herself, the oak tree was magnificent. All the other trees in the forest were wilted and their branches were almost bare with only a few leaves left hanging on from the harsh winter.

As Hannah got nearer to the oak tree her hands began to tingle like pins and needles, but as she looked down there was a swirl of golden dust forming around the palm of her hands, she gasped in shock and stumbled backwards, watching, fascinated, as the golden dust magically swirled around her arms and legs before dancing over towards the oak tree. She got to her feet, and then saw what she had been looking for all along...

'Alfie!' she squealed in excitement as she leapt over towards him. He neighed and jumped off from all four feet, before racing towards Hannah. She held her hands out to him as he bundled her over and began to nuzzle her pockets.

'Where have you been?' Hannah began to cry, but this time tears of relief. She was so happy to have found him. She could feel the bond so strongly. Suddenly, they were both surrounded by golden dust. Hannah gasped and looked at Alfie, who was once again bucking and squealing as the dust surrounded his hooves.

This meant Alfie could see the dust too, and she glanced over to the oak tree which had flames of golden and silver swirls around the trunk and the leaves were now shining all different colours, luscious greens, peachy pinks and bright blues, the sunlight filtered down through the tree as waves of gold swirled around the ground below.

Hannah gently stood up and staggered towards the tree. Alfie followed and watched Hannah as she climbed on the trunk and gently placed her hand on it; everything went silent, the golden swirls were now gone and the leaves were back to the luscious green, the only sound was the light wind which whipped Hannah's brown hair across her cheek.

'Well, that's it then' Hannah sighed as she got Alfie's head collar over his nose and buckled it up. She began to walk down from the tree and Alfie let out a low whinny. She looked back at him, and the words she had seen last week were now once again carved into the bottom of the tree. Hannah gingerly headed over towards it, and bending down she touched the carved words and read them out loud...

*'Believe in magic and you will find it...'*

There was suddenly a huge gust of wind, knocking her over; the golden dust once again began to dance like waves around the oak tree, it was extraordinary. She couldn't believe her eyes. The golden dust once again danced and swirled around them both, as if a ribbon had tied them together.

*'It's about time you figured it out'*

Hannah looked towards the oak tree, 'Hello?' she called out, 'Has the tree just spoken to me?' she thought.

*'No of course the tree hasn't just spoken to you, that would be ridiculous!'*

Hannah gasped. 'Has it just read my thoughts?'. She began to stagger to her feet in fright and lead Alfie down the path, but he stopped, dug his heels into the ground and wouldn't move.

'Alfie come on, we have to go, come on' Hannah cried as the golden dust now began to swirl around his hooves.

*'No we don't have to go yet, I haven't explained anything'*

Hannah dropped Alfie's lead rope and stared at him; the golden dust was now twinkling around her feet and working its way up her body. Had Alfie just spoken to her...?

'Alfie..?' Hannah questioned as she kneeled down on the grassy floor around the bottom of the oak tree and looked at Little Alf.

*'It's me, Hannah. I'm talking to you. It's Alfie'.*

Hannah's eyes widened, her face became hot and clammy and her heart began to race. Her stomach was full of butterflies, but this time she was nervous and excited at the same time.

'I don't understand how you're talking to me, is this real?' Hannah whispered, not wanting anyone else to hear her.

*'Yes, it's the old oak tree, it's enchanted...'*

The oak tree suddenly began to twinkle.

*'The tree has been here for thousands of years, but will only ever reveal its magic when someone figures out the secret words...'*

**'Believe in magic and you will find it'** Hannah whispered.

The tree suddenly began to sway in the wind as the dust began to sparkle once again around the leaves, turning them all different colours.

*'That's why I came here to show you the tree. I knew you would figure it out'.*

Hannah giggled excitedly 'Can anyone else do this, talk to their pony I mean...?' Hannah asked.

*'The last person to figure out the enchanted oak tree was over two hundred years ago. There was a young girl who lived in a village near the forest, she often used to visit when the forest was roaming with wild horses. She found the tree after she fell one day and grazed her knee. The tree healed her wounds and when she woke up she was surrounded by horses. She knew that when she fell her knee was covered in blood, but when she woke up it was as if nothing had happened, she was determined to come back every day and figure out what mystery it held'*

'How come nobody else knew about the tree? Why didn't she tell anyone?' Hannah asked.

*'You have to believe in magic to find it, and very few people believe in magic in today's world, you also have to have a very special connection with a horse, just like you and me'*

'Wow... so did the girl of two hundred years ago have a bond with a special horse?' Hannah's eyes began to gleam with excitement.

*'She had a bond with a particular wild foal in the forest. He was a young foal whose mother had been killed, and she helped raise him until he grew up and began to run with a herd of wild horses'.*

'So the legends are true, wild horses did used to roam the forest' Hannah gasped as she realised this.

'*Yes, horses ruled the forest for thousands of years, but when the forest was taken over by other wildlife and humans the horses began to fade, they were captured and used for people to ride*'

'So the herd vanished' Hannah whispered.

'*Yes it did, but the tree has always been here waiting for someone to discover its true magic...*'

'HANNAH! HANNAH!' a voice shouted.

Hannah jumped up quickly and searched for the voice calling her, she quickly turned towards the tree just in time to notice that all the glitter and dust she had just seen was gone... and Alfie was gently grazing next to her feet. She looked down at her yellow wellingtons and noticed there was no hint of mud on them. She began to walk, and then noticed her ankle was no longer throbbing and the bruise had vanished from her arm. Hannah grinned; she knew the tree had healed her and it wasn't a dream.

'Hannah, is that you?' a voice was now emerging from the nearby trees.

'Yeah, it's me! I found Alfie!' Hannah shouted back as she began to lead Alfie towards the voice.

'Oh thank God! You're okay, it's 4 o' clock, we were meant to meet at two but you never showed up, so we've been searching for you and Alfie. Your parents are so worried. I'll phone them now, they thought something must have happened to you' said the man, who had been among the team searching for Alfie that morning.

 Hannah looked confused. 'How can it be 4 o'clock?', she thought to herself, she had found Alfie straight away this morning, that would mean she had been by the enchanted tree for six hours... She looked at the tree one last time, before heading into the forest and back to Meadowlea Stables.

# Chapter Eight

There was a loud cheer as Hannah emerged from the forest with Alfie, Hannah's parents rushed over to hug her and stroke Alfie, they were so pleased to see them back safe.

'I knew he would be around somewhere, where did you find him?' questioned Ruth.

'Oh... he was just in the woods eating some grass... I think he must have got lost or something...' said Hannah, grinning.

'Well at least you're back now! You must be freezing. How about you put Alfie in his stable and we'll all have a nice hot drink in the stables kitchen' Hannah's Mum said.

'Great idea' said Hannah, as she began to head back to Alfie's stable. When she got back she gave Alfie a massive hug; she was so pleased to see him, but now she had discovered Alfie's secret, she couldn't wait to go back to the forest tomorrow and see what other tales Alfie had to tell her. Alfie nuzzled her pockets as Hannah crouched down to tickle his mane.

'I hope you never ever go missing again Alfie, even if it *is* to show me the enchanted tree...' Hannah said, as she yawned.

***

'ALFIE, ALFIE!' Hannah screamed as she bolted up, panicking, before realising she was in her bedroom at home.

'What's the matter, Hannah?' said her Dad as he rushed in to her room looking very sleepy.

'Is Alfie okay?' Hannah asked, surprised to find that she was at home. Had it all been a dream?

'Yes! He's in his stable, but you fell asleep against the stable door so we carried you to the car' sighed her Dad.

Hannah let out a huge sigh of relief 'Sorry I panicked. I must have been really tired to fall asleep in the stable!'

'Well you didn't sleep last night, and you were out in the forest looking for Alfie all day so that will probably explain things! When we found you in his stable asleep, Alfie was watching you the whole time' said her Dad. Hannah giggled before she fell back to sleep...

\*\*\*

It wasn't until Hannah woke up the next day that she really realised what had happened in the enchanted forest. 'Alfie could talk to me!' she hummed inside her head as she headed down the yard towards Alfie's stable. It was a sunny peaceful December morning at the stables without a cloud in the sky, there was no noise apart from the leaking tap outside the old barn, and Hannah was the first person to be out on the yard. She gently creaked open the wooden barn and was met with whinnies from the horses who had been in their stables overnight.

As she headed down to Alfie's stable, all the horses popped their heads over the doors to greet her, and Hannah stroked each of their soft noses. Paddy began to kick his door waiting to be fed when Hannah reached his stable.

'Paddy! Don't be so impatient, it's only seven o'clock, nobody's here yet' Hannah said, giggling as she sneakily fed Paddy a carrot from her pocket.

There was a huge whinny as Hannah gently tiptoed towards Alfie's stable; she peered over the stable door to see Alfie patiently waiting for her to open the door.

'Hello Alfie' she said. He jumped forward, startled by Hannah's voice.

She gently opened his door and Alfie let out a low whinny, she crouched down and stroked his fluffy face as Alfie began to nuzzle her pockets, Hannah giggled.

'That tickles' she said as Alfie was now trying to pinch the carrots through her pocket!

'I thought I heard someone creeping around this morning'

'Ah', Hannah screamed and stumbled backwards! Startled by the voice, she landed on the sawdust in Alfie's stable.

'Oops, sorry Hannah I didn't mean to scare you! I thought you would have heard the door go' Ruth said, grinning. Hannah looked up and noticed Ruth was still in her pyjamas.

'Sorry I didn't mean to wake you up! I just came to see Alfie and maybe take some photos when the sun rises' Hannah said, happily.

'Do your parents know you're here? It's still early?' Ruth questioned.

'Of course they do! Dad dropped me off this morning before he went to work!' Hannah said.

'Oh good. Just had to check. People usually start to arrive around 8:30 –9:00 am now that it's the Christmas holidays!' Ruth beamed.

'I know! I'm so excited for Christmas!' Hannah giggled, and Alfie snorted! 'I think Alf is too!'

Ruth and Hannah laughed as Alfie shook his head in excitement.

'Well when you do go outside it might be best you stick to the ménage today, I'm afraid we won't be able to go into the mysterious forest anymore' Ruth sighed.

'Why?' Hannah said, thinking about the enchanted tree.

'They're chopping down the trees, remember, to make room for building' Ruth replied.

'No they can't! Hannah cried, she had forgotten all about the woods being chopped down. 'What about the enchanted tree?' Hannah thought to herself; she may never be able to talk to Alfie again.

'I know it is such a shame, there were protected documents in the Library against the forest, but since the fire nobody is sure what they really said' Ruth said, sadly.

Hannah began to get upset, she couldn't let the forest be chopped down, the enchanted tree had been there for thousands of years and it was the only way she could talk to Alfie... she had only found the magic in the woods yesterday. Hannah knew she had to go in to the woods and try and figure out what to do even though Ruth had told her not to... Maybe Alfie would know... it was her only hope...

# Chapter Nine

'Believe in magic and you will find it...'

Hannah whispered as she stood next to the big solid oak tree with Little Alf by her side.

Once again the tree began to change, the magic of the branches glittered and twinkled in the sun, the dust was glimmering and began to fall from the tree and swirl to the ground creating a bed of gold dust beneath the roots of the trees.

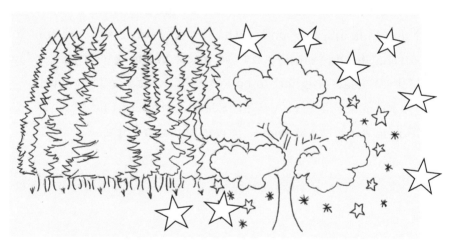

The leaves once again changed colour and sparkled just like a rainbow in the sun. The golden dust began to dance around the tree and Hannah watched in amazement as it began to circle her and Alfie... There was a sudden large burst of light and Hannah squinted to try and see what happening....

'Alfie' Hannah whispered... 'Alfie...'

Hannah began to panic. Why wasn't Alfie answering? She looked down to see him still happily standing next to her, almost waiting for something to happen. Then there was a huge burst of light which soared through the forest, a huge rumble ran underneath Hannah's feet; she stared, shocked. 'That's never happened before' she thought to herself. 'What was that...? ' she whispered as she glanced around the forest, everything quiet.

*'The enchanted tree is waking up'*

'Alfie!' Hannah squealed relieved to hear Alfie once again.

*'Hello, Hannah'*

She smiled, still overwhelmed with everything, but she knew why she had come to the forest today.

'Alfie, the forest is going to be chopped down, the enchanted tree will be gone forever, how will I ever be able to talk to you? It's not fair' Hannah said, suddenly becoming very upset, she couldn't bear the thought of not being able to talk to him.

*'There are documents in the library that will help you. Documents about old legends which are protecting the forest'*

Hannah sighed. 'Everyone knows about the documents. They got caught up in the fire, so there are no longer records of the forest or the land surrounding it'.

*'There is a very old book in the back of the library, it will be very worn by now, but it wasn't in the fire, and that will save the forest. You have to go and find it'*

'Are you sure?' Hannah said uncertainly. If the book was still there then why had nobody come across it yet...?

*'Yes, but you have to hurry, they are going to start chopping down the forest tomorrow, and if they managed to uproot any of the trees the magic could be lost forever...'*

Hannah gasped, so many questions still whirled through her brain, but she knew she had to save the forest, she began to move swiftly. Alfie followed her as they headed back to Meadowlea. She hoped that she would be able to speak to Alfie again soon.

'Hannah! Alfie! ' a voice shouted.

Hannah turned around to see Rusty, the owner of Colliwath stables, emerging from the forest riding her horse, Ryan.

'Hi!' Hannah shouted, as Rusty trotted Ryan towards her.

'What are you doing here? You do know the forest is going to be chopped down soon, they've been railing it all off today to make sure no one enters, it's not safe. Does Meadowlea Stables know?' Rusty questioned.

'Yeah I know... I just wanted to visit it for the last time' Hannah said quickly, hoping she wouldn't ask any more questions. She knew Ruth had told her specifically not to go into the forest today.

'Me too, I took Ryan around the cross country course for one last time before they chop it down. He loves cross country! Although he still thinks he's jumping the hurdles at the racecourse sometimes. Recently one of my stable girls Carla has been teaching him dressage!' said Rusty.

'Wow! That's amazing, I've always wanted to learn dressage, it looks so elegant' Hannah said, fascinated.

'Well if you ever want to come with me and Carla we often take the horses to weekend events at Richmond Equestrian Centre!' Rusty said.

'Really, that will be fantastic!' Hannah said.

Ryan began to prance and snort at Little Alf, clearly wondering why there was a horse so small.

'Well, that's my cue to go!' said Rusty as she said goodbye and cantered down the field. Hannah quickly glanced at her watch, and continued her journey back towards the stables. She had to get to the library today... and fast.

As soon as she got back she quickly put Alfie in his stable and kissed him on his nose. It was starting to get dark in the winter months, Hannah had phoned her Mum on the way back and asked if they could visit the library, her Mum had agreed as she needed to return some cookbooks but they couldn't stay long, Hannah hoped that the book she needed was in an obvious place or the forest could be lost forever...

Hannah heard her Mum outside, and shouted goodbye to Alfie as she rushed out.

'Whoa, why're you in such a hurry?' her mum asked.

'Oh, I just need to get to the library in plenty of time' Hannah replied.

'Well we can't stay long, I need to get back before your brother does as I have the house key' said Mum.

'Okay' Hannah said, hoping she would have enough time.

***

Once she had entered the library she knew it was going to be difficult, all of the books looked colourful and modern and there were rows and rows of them set out in categories. She let out a groan; this was going to be far more difficult than she had thought.

'Can I help you with anything?' the short plump lady, who was now looking at Hannah through her small rounded spectacles, asked.

'Well... I'm looking for an old book' Hannah replied, uncertain what the book looked like.

'Aren't you a little bit too young to be reading and handling old books?' the lady asked, looking suspiciously at Hannah.

'Ermm... No I'm studying old books at school, I find them very interesting' Hannah said, hoping the lady thought she was telling the truth.

'Very well then, if you follow me we have some this way' the lady said as she began to walk down the library.

Hannah followed the lady through a small arch which led into a tall round room. The cabinets were all dark wood and the floor was made of a dark, almost black, marble, she was amazed that she had never seen this room in the library before.

'This is the only part of the old building which remains; the rest of it was lost in a fire' the lady said, before heading back to a customer who stood waiting patiently by the till. Hannah circled the room fascinated. How was she going to find the book tonight? She sighed. She began to search for the book when something caught her eye...

A small glow seemed to come from underneath one of the cabinets, but as Hannah got nearer she realised it was actually coming from underneath an old door. She could tell that the door was old; she hadn't noticed it when she first entered the room.

'Why hadn't the lady mentioned it?' she muttered to herself.

As Hannah got closer to the door she realised how old it must be. Scratches edged their way along the bottom of the door and the corners were uneven and cracked, the door knob hung loose, as if waiting for someone to step inside.

Hannah gently pushed the door, it slowly creaked open scraping the floor beneath... she was hit with a layer of dust. It was obvious that nobody had entered the room for years, Hannah squinted as her eyes adjusted to the dark. This room was again full of different books but much smaller; the ceiling was cracked and there were huge puddles of water where the rain had managed to leak in.

Hannah began to search the room; the books were big and heavy and covered in dust and old cobwebs. She had been searching for over fifteen minutes, and she knew her Mum would soon come looking for her. At that moment there was a twinkle of magic dust along the bookshelf by the old fire, and Hannah knew she had found the book.

The black leather book shone as the dust sparkled around it. It was fatter than the others and stood a couple of inches higher. As soon as she touched it she knew this was the right book. There was the same magical feeling running through Hannah's body as she had felt in the forest. She pulled the book out of the shelf; it was surprisingly light and very smooth for such a hard object. Hannah was hit by a musty smell as she began to open the pages...

'Hannah, where are you? We have to go, your brother's at home already!'

'Oh no' Hannah muttered. She hadn't opened the book yet, she quickly placed it in her bag and slowly creaked open the door.

'Hannah! Where are you?' Mum shouted again.

'Sorry Mum, just coming' Hannah said as she quickly grabbed one of the other books off the shelf. She didn't want the lady from the library knowing about the room she had found.

'Oh there you are, look at your jeans! Why are you covered in dust?!' asked her Mum.

'It's dusty in there' Hannah replied.

'Well come on, we'd best go! I think we'll have to come back for the book another time, sorry Hannah' her Mum said.

'Oh never mind' Hannah said, grinning. She had the book she wanted, and couldn't wait to see what it had inside. It was her last hope to save the forest...

# Chapter Ten

As soon as Hannah got home, she ran upstairs. She wanted to know what secrets the book was hiding, and, jumping on her bed, she began to eagerly unzip her rucksack to reveal the black leather book. She was nervous as she began to turn the first page and was hit with the same musty smell she had experienced in the library.

As she turned the first dusty page she was met with a huge drawing of a herd of wild horses, Hannah gasped, it was so beautiful. The drawing was full of colour and life. Although the page was yellow and faded it was still possible to see each detail of the horses. The first drawing was of a huge majestic black stallion with muscles rippling down his neck and a glossy flowing mane and tail. There were at least twenty horses behind the stallion, Golden Palominos, athletic thoroughbreds, stocky Gypsy Cob and Shire horses, all full of grace and beauty. Hannah could even make out the small miniature Shetland at the back of the herd looking cheeky; she smiled as it reminded her of Little Alf.

'Could it be a relative of little Alf's?' she thought to herself. She still had so many questions to ask Little Alf about how he had first come to the forest and whether he had always lived there.

The next page was full of writing and numbers. She carefully began to scan the page looking for any clues which might help her with saving the forest, when she saw the words...

*'The meadow forest'*

'The meadow forest' she whispered to herself, this had to be the clue she was looking for, and underneath the words was a small drawing of a large oak tree. She began to read...

*'The meadow forest belongs to the wild horses which have roamed there for over 10,000 years. The forest is a paradise to allow the horses to roam free and wild, and has been preserved over the years for the horses that live there. In 1865 there was a small village attached to the forest where people would watch over the wild herds living on the land, although nobody has ever come into contact with them, as this would be too dangerous. The ancient woodland was signed over to Mr. L. C. Brown in 1965, where he would watch over the horses, allowing them to live freely on the land. In 1980 there were very few horses left after people had started to capture them and use them as riding horses. The only horses that remained were the young stallions and very few mares.'*

Hannah gasped. Did this mean the land had been sold again? She slowly turned over the next page which revealed an old tattered map of the forest which had frayed over the years. She began to study the map and realised it was an outline of the forest boundary.

'Hannah it's time for bed now, turn your light off please!' she heard her Dad shout from downstairs.

Hannah glanced at the clock and groaned; it was already 9:30pm and she still had the whole of the book to read... She turned her light off and gently tiptoed back into bed; she dived under the covers with her torch and began to read the rest of the book...

*'It was once said that a girl had fallen in the forest and when she woke up the horses had surrounded her, protecting her from the other creatures that lived in the forest'*

Hannah stopped reading, was this what Alfie had explained to Hannah yesterday about the other girl being able to talk with horses, and was this the other girl who had also discovered the tree...?

She was halfway through the book and still hadn't found any clues as to what could help her save the forest, and time was running out. She carefully flashed her torch at her alarm clock to reveal it was now 12:30 am. Hannah yawned as she began to read the rest of the pages...

Hannah had given up all hope as she turned the last page. She had found out secrets she didn't know, facts and who had owned the forest at certain parts over the years but the book had ended suddenly, as if there were parts missing. She sighed to herself and soon began to feel very sad; she was going to lose the one gift she had recently discovered. She carefully placed the book on her bedside cabinet and crawled under her covers.

'At least I'll still have Alfie' she thought to herself as she yawned again. Just as she started to close her eyes she saw something sparkle...

# ★ Chapter Eleven

Hannah swiftly crawled out of bed. The book had dropped off the cabinet and landed on the floor. ☆

'That's odd' she whispered, she hadn't heard the book fall off the cabinet. She delicately picked up the book, not wanting to tear any of the pages, she carefully studied it to see golden dust now dancing around the bottom of a worn page, the frayed yellow page was blank but in one of the corners small words were beginning to form...

Believe in magic and you will find it.

*'Believe in magic and you will find it'*

Hannah gently began to smooth the page with her hand and whispered the words once again...

'Believe in magic and you will find it.'

Nothing happened. She whispered the words again, more clearly this time, but still nothing happened. She frowned. When she had said the words before something had always happened, but this time there was silence throughout the house, and she realised that it was perhaps because she wasn't next to the enchanted tree. Suddenly, small stars began to form along the bottom of the page, they looked like snowflakes but she knew they were stars by the way they glowed against the paper.

Hannah was puzzled, what could this mean? She slowly began to move the page over as the dust began to dance around the page once again. Once the dust had settled it gathered along a small edge...

'A secret pocket' Hannah smiled. She had a very good feeling about what she was going to find. She gingerly slid her hand inside the secret pocket and pulled out a very dusty piece of brown paper. She opened it...

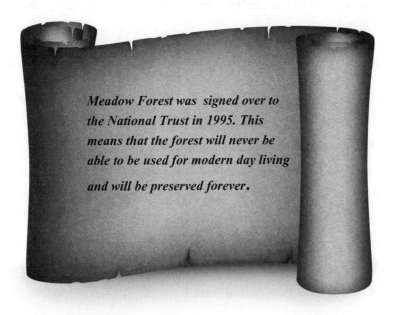

*Meadow Forest was signed over to the National Trust in 1995. This means that the forest will never be able to be used for modern day living and will be preserved forever.*

Hannah laughed. She couldn't believe it! She had found the answer she had been looking for. She remembered her parents signing up for the National Trust the year before, and her Grandad had explained to her that the Trust saved and preserved patches of land forever. She slept peacefully that night, knowing she had found a way to save the enchanted forest.

\*\*\*

A whinny ran out as Hannah arrived at the stables; she knew it was Alfie before she had even got into the barn. Alfie had a very high-pitched whinny and she could always tell it apart from all the other horses. She ran down to his stable clutching the black leather book and the documents she had found the night before.

'Hello Alfie' Hannah beamed as she opened his stable door.

Alfie shuffled towards the door and held his nose up waiting for Hannah to kiss him on the nose. Hannah giggled as she put Alfie's head collar on and headed towards Ruth's office. She couldn't wait to show her the documents. She skipped happily up to the stables office with Alfie trotting by her side, the cold winter's morning was peaceful, there was a slight breeze which swept his mane making it flow in the wind; the only sound to be heard was the cars whizzing by in the distance as people hurried to their morning's work.

Hannah was just about to open the office door when she heard a loud bang and something scrambling in the distance. She swiftly turned round to see there were diggers, tractors and large machinery heading across the fields towards the forest.

'Oh no, they're early!' she shouted, and quickly began to knock on the office door.

'Ruth's round in the hay barn!' she heard a voice shout, she quickly turned round to see Tilly coming out of the ménage, riding Jack.

'Well quickly, we need to find her!' Hannah shouted, panicking. Alfie began to snort and prance on the spot nervously.

'Why, has something happened?' Tilly asked, puzzled.

'No… well - yes… I've found a way to save the forest, but we have to hurry, they're about to chop it down!' Hannah cried as she began to run down towards the hay barn with Alfie bolting ahead. She ran into the hay barn and slammed into the large man wearing a hard hat, who was standing talking to Ruth; she stumbled backwards and landed in the straw below.

'Whoa, calm down Hannah, what's the matter?' Ruth asked, as Hannah scrambled to her feet.

'The forest can't be chopped down!' Hannah said, out of breath.

'Well it can, and they're about to start. I've come here to warn you about how noisy it's going to be' said the large man. Hannah realised he must be one of the managers who was in charge of chopping down the forest.

'No it can't. I have documents to say that it's rightfully owned by the National Trust and nobody can touch it because it has to be preserved' Hannah said proudly, as Alfie snorted. Ruth looked at Hannah questioningly. 'Have you seen these documents before?' he asked Ruth. Ruth struggled for words 'I'm not sure…' she raised her eyebrow, looking at Hannah.

Hannah opened up the black leather book and carefully picked up the worn page and passed it to the man who was now staring at her suspiciously. She watched as his eyes flicked over the piece of paper, he held it for a minute re-reading the words before grunting and handing it back.

'Where did you find that document?' the man asked, frowning.

'In the library last night' Hannah gulped as she answered.

'It doesn't prove anything, the build will still be going ahead and the tree's will still be chopped down.' the man said.

***

'No it won't!' a voice said behind Hannah.

Hannah swiftly turned around to see there was another man also wearing a hard hat standing behind her. 'Another worker from the forest', Hannah thought, and noticed that Tilly was next to him smiling at Hannah and holding her thumbs up.

'Let me look at them documents' he asked, Hannah handed them over. The man swiftly scanned over the documents before clearing his throat.

'Well it seems to me that we will be stopping the trees from being chopped down. Bob, you ring the other workers' said the man.

'But we already have the equipment on site' the man began to argue.

'Ring them now. That's an order' the man said.

Hannah cheered, Alfie bucked, and Ruth and Tilly began to giggle.

'I've always loved that forest. My Great Grandma used to tell me stories about the wild horses which used to roam the land, and she once told me a very secret story when I was only young about a special oak tree. I went looking for it but never found it. I suppose the stories weren't real though' the man said.

Hannah looked at the man strangely before realising his Grandma must have been the other girl from years ago, the other girl who had also believed in magic and discovered the oak tree's secrets. ★

# Chapter Twelve

Hannah sat on the grassy bank and watched as the last of the heavy machinery headed back towards the road and away from the forest.

'We saved it, Alfie' Hannah said as she stroked his ears. Alfie gently rested his muzzle on Hannah's lap and softly breathed against her legs.

'Well that was certainly a surprise' Tilly said happily, sitting down next to Hannah and gently stroking Alfie's fluffy neck.

Hannah giggled. 'Well I couldn't stand the thought of losing the forest forever, it's where I found Alfie after all'

'I knew you must have found something! I rode Jack over to the forest workers and told them to stop building' said Tilly.

'You did that?' Hannah asked as Alfie began to munch the last of the grass which was still peeping through the frost.

'Of course I did! It was like the time we found Alfie. I knew something must have happened!' said Tilly.

Hannah hugged Tilly 'Thank you so much! If that man hadn't come over, the forest might not be there now' Hannah said.

Clouds were now beginning to form in the sky and there was a light flicker of snow gently beginning to glisten and land on the frosty ground. Hannah gently got up and began to tug

Alfie back towards his stable, but he wouldn't budge. She looked at him, puzzled.

'What's wrong?' she said as she patted his mane.

Alfie then began to snort and hoof the snow, before getting down and rolling! Hannah quickly grabbed her camera and began to take photos as she watched Alfie kicking and bucking through the snow!

***

Hannah happily closed Alfie's stable door as he stood munching his hay with his bright yellow stable rug on, she couldn't believe they had managed to save the forest and she couldn't wait for all the exciting adventures with Alfie yet to come. She glanced back towards Alf as a twinkle of golden dust swirled around his stable. She giggled as she shut the barn door...

The magic is just beginning...

Look out for the 3rd book as Hannah and Little Alf encounter more magical events...

# Little Alf Gallery

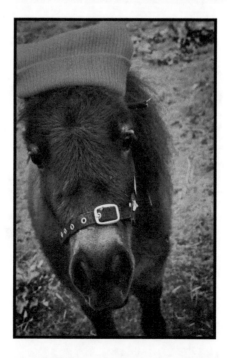

## About the Author & Little Alf!

Hannah Louise Russell published her first book in 2014 at the young age of 17. 'The Magical Adventure of Little Alf- The discovery of the wild pony' - was the first book in the 'Little Alf' series.

After publishing her first book, Hannah decided to design a clothing range exclusive to Little Alf. This now has a wide variety of children's and adult's clothing, which can be found at: www.littlealf.com

Then, at the start of 2015 Hannah has published this, her second book in the series

### 'The Magical Adventure of Little Alf – The Enchanted Forest'

Hannah and Little Alf help support the Riding for the Disabled Association through the work they do. Hannah is an active volunteer at her local Riding for the Disabled Centre and Little Alf occasionally goes to visit too. Hannah Russell is the owner of Little Alf, who lives happily behind her house in the North Yorkshire Dales, and is usually found creating mischief in his home .

The reason Hannah decided to write a series on Little Alf is because he is completely different from other Miniature Shetlands as he is a mini mini mini mini Shetland due to little Alf having dwarfism.

Therefore this makes him super tiny, as well as being super cute! Hannah and little Alf have a very special bond and are never found far apart.

Since publishing her first book in 2014, Hannah and Little Alf have started a tour visiting local agricultural shows, performing in the main ring and travelling to book signings together! If you follow them on their blog you will be able to see which destination they are visiting next! Come meet Little Alf up close and get your book signed!

Little Alf brings Hannah great happiness and joy, as she hopes he will to other people too, as they experience the magic of these stories....

*Hannah & Little Alf*

*X*

# Little Alf and the Riding for the Disabled Association

Little Alf helps support the Riding for the Disabled Association!

An Article from the RDA

When Hannah Russell brought her miniature Shetland pony to Bedale Group RDA he was a huge hit with our riders. Little Alf suffers from dwarfism so at 28 inches high, he is tiny, even for a miniature Shetland. Hannah's book "The Magical Adventure of Little Alf " is helping to raise funds for RDA, and Hannah is now one of our group volunteers on a Thursday morning. Students from the Dales School met Alf and realised how much of a character he is. The book reflects this and five further books are planned. Next year Little Alf will be going to the Royal Horse Show but he will always be welcome at Bedale Group RDA where we try to build riders' confidence and increase mobility whilst enjoying riding. You can follow the adventures of Little Alf at his blog www.littlealf.com & you may soon see him too on our website www.rdabedalegroup.org.uk

If any group would like a visit from Little Alf, please contact Hannah through their web site.

# Meet the horses and ponies from the book!

## Paddy!

One of the main characters! This is Paddy - Hannah's gypsy cob.

Paddy did not have the best start in life, but he is now living happily with Hannah and enjoys their rides out around their home!

Paddy is lovable, cheeky, playful and of course, gorgeous!

Hannah takes Paddy to lots of shows in hand. In 2014 they came 3rd in a North regional CHAPS show!

## Badger!

Badger was featured mostly in the first book but also has a few scenes in the second!

Badger was Hannah's first pony and she has now owned him for over 11 years! Badger is currently retired and loves his life mooching around the field! He still lives with Hannah.

Hannah use to take Badger to pony club every Saturday!

## Pepper!

Pepper is featured in the first and second book as Badger's companion!

Badger and Pepper have been the best of buddies for ten years and they are usually found in the field together!

And of course the main character!

## Little Alf

Fact File

Name : Little Alf

Age : 2 years old.

Date of birth: 1st April 2012

Loves : playing with Hannah! ☺ Meeting new people!

Dislikes: Rain and cold weather

(He screams to come to bed if it rains!)

Little Alf has an online website where he has his own shop, blogs, videos, news page and much more!

# www.littlealf.com